Last Left Standing

Last Left Standing

Barbara T. Russell

Houghton Mifflin Company
Boston 1996

For information about this and other Houghton Mifflin trade
and reference books and multimedia products, visit
The Bookstore at Houghton Mifflin on the World Wide Web
at http://www.hmco.com/trade/.

Manufactured in the United States of America
The text of this book is set in 14 pt. Dante
BP   10   9   8   7   6   5   4   3   2   1

Library of Congress Cataloging-in-Publication Data

Russell, Barbara T.
Last left standing / by Barbara T. Russell.
p.   cm.
Summary: Through his friendship with an elderly woman and her
granddaughter, Josh comes to terms with his brother's death.
ISBN 0-395-71037-5
[1. Death — Fiction. 2. Brothers — Fiction.]
I. Title.
PZ7.R91536Las   1996   94-16732
[Fic] — dc20   CIP   AC

To my mother and father

Last Left Standing

1

A House in the Groves

Josh knew it wasn't right to listen to what other people said in private, especially when those people were his momma and daddy. He figured he had it coming when the blue hydrangea beneath their window soaked his shirt with morning dew, but it didn't stop him from pressing his ear to the wall planks. He just had to know if they ever talked about Toby anymore, like they used to when they were in bed at night and Josh and Toby snuck out to listen from the hallway.

"He's gone off again, Lib," Daddy said. "Where do you think he goes all day?"

Josh heard the covers rustle. He could imagine Momma sitting up in bed in her pink nightgown, with that little comma she got between her eyes when something bothered her.

"He'll be back," she said. A minute later, her hand appeared and released the spring shade at the window. Josh had to press tight to the peeling boards of the house to keep from being seen. "He generally shows up by suppertime, but I can't figure why. He won't eat. Have you seen how thin he's gotten? Tries to hide it wearing Toby's big shirts."

"Now, Libby." Josh heard his father's voice soften. "Things will get better when school starts. He's going to get over this. We all will."

"Will we?" Josh could tell by Momma's voice that the little comma had not gone away. "I wish I were so sure."

Josh bolted across the road and into the

shelter of the orange groves. He wouldn't duck under the window again. He had heard enough.

The plows had been through the orange groves over the weekend, leaving the dirt high between the trees. Josh took off his shoes and tied them to his belt loops before he moved on.

The blue jays called from tree to tree, and the sun splintered through the branches and angled thin little spotlights onto the ground. Sweat dripped off the tips of Josh's hair and down his jaw, but he didn't bother to wipe it away.

"JOSHHH!" Daddy's voice rose from somewhere behind him. Josh was at least a half-dozen rows inside the grove, but his father's voice reminded him to keep up his pace.

"JOSH!"

For a minute, Josh hesitated. He wished they wouldn't worry about him. Momma especially. She was home all day while Daddy was working at the cabinet shop.

It was hard to stay in that house. He knew. Toby's stuff was all there. Sometimes, if he let himself go numb, Josh could imagine Toby was off at camp like last summer, counselor in training, only this time Toby was staying for the long session.

"Josh, did you hear me?" his father called.

Yeah. He heard. But he had forced his legs into a run and now they wouldn't stop for anything. If legs could run away from quiet, he knew that's what his were doing. Without Toby, that house on the other side of the road was like a tomb.

Toby woke up noisy. Mattress creaking, water hissing from the tap, the Cougar fight song ringing through the house once the shower door banged shut.

Then, "Ta-da." He bounced into the kitchen. "Welcome to the Toby Harding Comedy Hour. Televised from the original home of the Crazies. Let's go over and say a big hello to the two head crazies, John and Libby Harding," he'd say, holding a banana under Momma's and Daddy's faces.

Daddy would shake his head at Momma, but they'd smile at each other as though they shared a secret.

When they turned to him, Josh would smile, too, knowing the secret was how goofy Toby was and how he could make the whole house practically vibrate with his loud, lunatic ways.

"JOSH!" It was Daddy's voice again, but this time it sounded closer, as if he might have crossed to the edge of the grove to look for him. He'd started doing that lately.

Josh ducked under tangles of branches. He couldn't run between the rows of orange trees. It would be too easy to track exactly where he'd been in the soft dirt.

The leaves hung down to the ground, and Josh had to shoulder through them, almost like he was passing through one green room after another. He ran as fast as he could down to the barbwire Mr. Klein put up.

The last time old man Klein caught Toby and Josh past this fence, he had told them to stay clear of his land, but now Josh didn't care what he'd say. He hopped the fence, took a hard right, and ran farther than he ever thought he could without giving out.

Toby used to have to run alongside Josh the four circles around the track, shouting and cheering the whole way, to get Josh to run a mile. Today, Josh figured, he had almost doubled that.

He had never been in this part of the groves before, so when he stopped he took a minute to get his bearings. Toby had told him once that it was swampy on this side of the lake, but Josh didn't see anything like that. Just more orange trees stretched as far as he could see.

The sun was above the branches. Josh couldn't hear any sound but the quarrel of blue jays and mockingbirds, so he hunched over to catch his breath. A few minutes later, he stood up, started to whistle. He felt almost peaceful. The whole day lay ahead of him. He started walking again, slower this time, his head spinning from the long run and no food.

Then, there it was. Just like somebody took it from one place and slipped it into another. A little road that veered off from the groves and wound through a stand of pines. The orange trees around the road were scraggly, with wide spaces between them, as if they had to make room for something else, as if that road were their limit.

Josh startled as the sound of hammering

broke the silence. He darted from tree to tree trying to see what was at the end of the road.

Ahead, he saw a sunny clearing where somebody had planted cabbage and strawberries and string beans. A little shack was set up behind it, no bigger than a cottage.

At first he didn't see her, the sunlight was so bright, and the porch so shaded. He heard her first, singing some little tune. It sounded like a church hymn. Then he saw a tall, thin woman watering marigolds up at the porch rail.

"You coming out from there or you just going to spy all day?" The woman didn't look up from what she was doing.

Josh tightened himself into a line behind a wormy pine at the edge of the yard.

"You're bigger than that little old tree, you know. I can see you plain. You've got on a red plaid shirt and your hair's too long."

Josh eased out into view, his hands jammed into his back pockets. "Hey there," he said.

"Hey, yourself. What are you doing around here? Come on over where I can get a look at you." The woman jerked her head to one side and folded her arms over her chest as if Josh better do what she told him.

As he walked toward her, Josh tried to keep his eyes to the ground, but he couldn't help peeking a time or two at the woman's hair. It was gray all right, but not as dull as his grandma's. It had these glimmers in it, like the mica bits in the silt down by the lake.

"Now, you see that sign over there?" the old lady asked when he got right in front of her. Her eyes were brown as cowhide, and bright, even though she was maybe sixty.

He looked in the direction where she nod-ded. A big sign was nailed to the wormy pine he had hidden behind. It read NO TRESPASSING: TRESPASSERS WILL BE PROSECUTED.

When he looked back she raised her eyebrows as though she wanted an explanation, but he couldn't think of one, so he kept his mouth shut.

"What's your name, boy? I think your folks ought to know you're snooping around on private property."

Josh blinked. He sure didn't want Daddy checking up on him. "I ain't going to tell you. Sorry," he added, as if that would help.

The old woman looked at him hard and narrowed her eyes again. "Well, in that case, you better come in and explain before I decide you're nothing but a thief."

He felt his stomach burning under his shirt, and he wondered how fast he could run into the cover of the trees.

Then a shadow fell where the woman

stood, and a girl stepped out. Her hair had the same sparkly bits as the woman's, but hers was reddish and yellowish at the same time. Her overalls were dusty and faded.

He couldn't see her face because her hand was up to shade her eyes, but he could see she was no older than he was, thirteen maybe, and what his Momma would call a slip of a girl. In her other hand she held a hammer, which dropped from her fingers as she walked toward him.

"Toby." She shook her head as though she were trying to figure something out. "Toby?"

Josh's knees went jellyish. He turned around, but no one was behind him. All at once he heard only the birds again.

"Who are you talking to?" His words came out fast and sharp. The girl shifted out of focus, and he wished he had eaten.

"Bess Ann, be still." The old lady held out a

hand to stop the girl from talking or coming closer. "It ain't Toby, honey. Can't you see?"

Josh suddenly realized the sun was too hot. For a minute, a black sheet closed over his eyes. Then, wanting to see that girl's face in such a bad way, he willed the black sheet away and took a good, long look at her. She had moved the hand above her eyes to cover her mouth.

"It is Toby." Her eyes were as blue as the border on his momma's china cups. "Toby, where have you been?"

Josh heard a whine inside his head. "Quit calling me that!"

The girl stepped back into the shadows and Josh saw the black sheet pull down as sure as a shade over a window.

2

Mattie and Bess Ann

Josh smelled onions frying. A blur of color wobbled before him.

When he was sure he was awake, the blur became a painting, a big one, of a girl's face.

"Well," a woman's voice said. "Speak of the devil."

Josh jerked his head to one side. The old woman from the porch sat in a chair beside the sofa where he lay.

"How're you feeling?" she asked. "I had a time trying to get you in the house. I would have worn my brace if I'd known folks were going to be dropping like flies around the place today." She held a hand to the small of her back, but there was a little smile in her eyes as she spoke. She wiped her hands down the front of a long apron she wore over her paint-splotched shirt and jeans.

"I didn't faint," Josh said. "Just . . . " His head hurt so bad, he was afraid he might black out again.

"Well," the old lady said. "The sun is mighty hot out there, Mr. No Name. Would have run out and brought your folks if I'd have found some identification."

He started to sit up, but she held up a hand to stop him.

"You've been out for hours. I was just fixing to go fetch a doctor." She set her hands on her knees. "I'm Mattie," she said. "McCall."

Josh studied her as well as he could, but his head was not quite clear. It seemed the heat from outside had seeped inside his brain and made it fuzzy.

"I'm not going to call your people," she said. She held up her hand like scouts do when they make a promise. "Just give me a name, that's all."

"Josh," he said.

"I'll get you some water, Josh."

Mattie disappeared into the next room and a face peeked around the corner. It was the girl from the yard. The one Mattie called Bess Ann. When she saw him looking back at her, she ran out the door and into the bright daylight.

"I'll be right out. I just have to turn these onions down," Mattie called. She came back into the room as the screen door slammed behind Bess Ann.

"Don't pay her any attention, boy. She's mistaken you for somebody else." Mattie handed him a mason jar of water.

Josh finished the water in one long gulp.

"You sure favor him. Our friend, I mean,"

Mattie said. "I can understand why Bess Ann mistook you. Maybe you know him." She sat down in the rocking chair and pushed into a gentle motion. "Harding's his last name. First name's Toby."

Hearing Mattie say Toby's name was like somebody jamming a finger into a bad bruise. Josh concentrated on a spider making its way along the windowsill.

"He's my brother."

As soon as he said it, Josh knew he should have said Toby *was* his brother. He knew he should have said so then, but it felt good not to.

"Well, what do you know?" Mattie slapped her palms against her thighs. "Toby has a brother. He never said."

"How do you know him?" Josh asked.

"He used to come around here every so often. Brought his harmonica and played for

Bess Ann and me. He could sniff out a coconut custard pie from about anywhere, I guess. The minute I pulled one out of the oven, we knew we could count on Toby showing up. How come we never saw you?"

Josh shrugged. "I don't know." His eyes wandered around the room.

It was bright, and the floor was painted as green as the groves he had come through. Round, braided rug. An easel set up in the corner. Paintings all over whitewashed walls. Josh took one look at all the paintbrushes in jars that lined the windowsills and bet if it weren't for the onions, the room would smell like mineral spirits.

"What's he been up to? One day he was building us a fence and then he never came back. It about broke Bess Ann up, too. She was getting real attached to him. She's like that, you know, Bess Ann. Real sweet thing, but a little slow in the head." She touched a finger to her temple. "We don't get many visitors back here, which don't bother me much. Different for her, though."

Josh nodded, and Mattie waved her hand as if she were shooing a fly.

"I bet that Toby has shoved out for the summer. Didn't even tell us he was going."

Josh looked at the picture again and recognized Bess Ann. He looked back at Mattie. Her face had gone soft waiting for his answer. Then it tightened. "He's all right, isn't he? I mean, he hasn't been sick or something?"

Josh could practically hear the blood pouring into his head. "No, he's not sick." He hated the way his voice sounded, all bright and dopey. "It's like you said — he's gone for the summer. Counselor. Camp Flat Rock. You heard of it? Right over the line in North Carolina." Words rolled out of his mouth. "He asked me to come by here and tell you since he had to leave in such a hurry."

Mattie relaxed. "I told Bess Ann it was something like that. Come on in here and let me fix you a bite. I bet you're half starved."

She motioned Josh to follow her into the tiny kitchen and opened an aqua-green refrigerator. "I figured he headed out of town, but I've got to tell you, we sure do miss him coming around."

Josh studied the room while Mattie laid a whole sliced ham and some bread on a wooden table.

Behind her, more cups of soaking brushes were crowded in with jars of wildflowers. Mail was stacked lopsided in a chair beside the door, and a skillet clock was half hidden on a wall of pinned-up paintings.

"Kind of a junk heap, isn't it?" Mattie said. "Lived-in, I like to try and convince myself."

Josh heard the sound of the radio from a back room, the singsong voice of the girl outside, and the chatter of chickens in the yard. Even the brush strokes on the painting seemed loud. Not like the house across the groves. The house with hardly a sound but the flutter of curtains in the breeze and the clink of dishes being set to dry in the rack beside the sink.

"I like lived-in," he said.

"I'd let you call your folks, but we don't have a phone. Never liked them. Too much trouble," Mattie said. "Now, tell me, why in the world didn't you just say you were Toby's brother when you showed up? You haven't blacked out like that before, have you?"

Josh thought fast. "I left my house this morning before I ate. Guess it made me lightheaded."

He had never seen a lady as old as Mattie

dressed so grubby. When she drew near she smelled of paint and lye soap.

"That was before we knew Toby's brother had come to pay us a call." She piled ham on a piece of white bread.

Josh stole a peek at the pictures that covered the walls. Some looked like a four year old did them, all red and yellow and green smears. His eyes drifted back to the picture of Bess Ann by the door.

"Do you like that one? I did it last spring. I never get tired of painting Bess Ann. It's as though her heart shines right through to her face, isn't it?"

She took down a bag of potato chips and stacked a handful on a paper plate alongside a dill pickle.

"That's how she is." Mattie looked down at her hands and turned them over, as if seeing them for the first time. "That's what Toby liked best about coming here, I think."

"What?" Josh heard his own voice, a little too loud. He turned his gaze to the painting again, this time not seeing it. "What did he like?"

"Bess Ann," Mattie said. "Called her an angel. You and Toby look so much alike that when I saw you back in the woods, I was fooled for a minute. Thought it was him, coming to surprise us."

She squinted at him, and Josh studied his reflection in the window. He guessed he did favor Toby. He had heard enough people say it. Even though Toby was two years older than Josh, they both had fine, dark hair, even darker eyes, and their mother's long nose.

"Wait," Mattie said. She turned from the counter where she crushed mint into two glasses of iced tea. "I thought it was mighty queer for you to show up now."

She picked up her tea so fast it spilled over the side. "I know why you've come."

Josh's eyes stayed glued to the window, but he felt a little twitch play inside his cheek. He prayed the old woman hadn't figured out Josh hadn't told her the whole truth about Toby.

"Go on," Mattie said. "Tell me."

Josh watched a drop leak down the side of her glass as she waited for him to answer, but he couldn't utter a sound. His heavy words were all used up.

"Well?" Mattie's brown eyes went dark and narrow. Like pinpoints or question marks. They were waiting for the truth, but Josh could only watch everything around him, as though it were happening to someone on TV. He lowered himself into the kitchen chair to see how it all turned out.

3

Toby's Fence

All at once, the ticking of the skillet clock sounded like a fast-dripping faucet.

"Toby has left it to you to finish that fence for him. Am I right?"

Josh concentrated on Mattie's mouth.

"Yep. That's right. I've come to finish the fence." A muscle twitched beside his mouth like it always did when he was nervous.

Her own lip had little lines around the top that disappeared when she laughed. "Hah. Knew it."

Josh decided Mattie's face seemed joyful, too, like Bess Ann's in the picture by the front door. Her smile was the pure kind they talk about in church. Not watered-down like most people's.

"That rascal." Mattie clicked her tongue and handed him the sweaty glass of tea. "Did he tell you it would take the better part of a week to get it done? I bet he didn't tell you that, now, did he?"

Josh laughed out loud.

"If you're feeling all right after you eat, I'll show you where everything is. You can make up your mind for yourself if you want the job. Bess Ann could help you."

As Josh wolfed down the sandwich, he watched Bess Ann out the kitchen window, chasing chickens in the back yard. Behind her was a shed, a chicken house with a broken board or two at the front. She ran past a long stretch of grass that sloped toward a strand of silvery lake.

"I told Bess Ann she could meet you proper after you feel rested," Mattie said.

Josh followed Mattie down the back stairs. The bright sun hurt his eyes and the smell of chickens gagged him, but it was nothing compared to the ache when Mattie showed him the fence posts that had been dug into the corner of the yard.

"This is it," Mattie said.

Josh ran his fingers over the first nail in the post. The head and neck of the nail stuck out of the wood and had been hammered off to the side. Toby had done the same thing on the tree house they built in the woods. He said it made a stronger bond if the nail was hammered in and then over like that.

Josh's knees went soft under him. "Toby did this."

"Sure did," Mattie said.

Josh squatted down, held on tight to the metal netting. He pretended to tie his shoe, his face pressed against the coolness of the wire, till his legs stopped rattling under him.

"You all right?" Mattie asked, her face gone funny again. "Now, if you don't want — "

"No." He shook his head. "I'm all right."

The fence was just a chicken-wire roll nailed into posts.

"You can see he didn't get far."

Josh figured he could finish the job in three or four days. He would have to now. Serve him right for not telling Mattie about Toby.

"Bess Ann just loves these silly chickens," Mattie whispered when they reached the chicken house. "Treats them like babies, that's for sure. But it's harmless, and we can sure use the egg money."

While Josh walked off the distance from the chicken house to the end of the yard, Bess Ann sat cross-legged in the dirt and watched. "You some kin of Toby's?"

Josh felt goose bumps again. "Yes."

"What's your name?" she asked, even though when she had shown him where the tools were kept, he had told her twice. When he looked in her eyes, Josh felt he could look down into the deepest part of her. Like the spring he found in the woods, her thoughts ran clear, not like the kids he knew, himself even, who had learned to muddy the water if they chose.

"Josh. Josh Harding."

"I'm worried about my chickens, Josh. They could wander out of the yard and get hurt. There's bobcats around here, you know."

"I've never seen one in this stretch," he said.

"But you'll finish the fence?" The lines on Bess Ann's forehead rose into a peak.

"I've got to ask my folks if it's okay, first," he told her, even though the last thing on

Josh's mind was telling Momma and Daddy about this place.

After he thanked Mattie for the sandwich and said goodbye, Josh cut through the woods and headed in the direction he had run that morning. When the little road stopped and the groves began, a tiredness fell over him as though he had traveled hours instead of minutes from Mattie and Bess Ann's house.

He was numb from the day. That's what he was. Numb and wide awake at the same time. Josh couldn't stop his mind from racing long enough to concentrate on getting home. Couldn't stop from thinking about Toby.

His mind ran off questions so quick they just piled up. How come Toby never told him about this place? They didn't keep secrets from each other. They were friends. Not like Ritzy and his little brother, James, who couldn't even sit in the same room without getting in a fight over who got the prize from the cereal box.

Ritzy and Toby had been friends since Ritzy moved to Lakeland in sixth grade. For the last couple of years, Josh had ridden on the same bus with them, been at the same school, gone along with them to the gym to play pick-up in the afternoons. But this September, Toby would have gone to high school with Ritzy while Josh stayed behind in junior high. Josh wondered what secrets might have been kept from him then.

Still it was hard to imagine Toby could keep a secret from anyone. Especially in the fall, when Toby's mouth went ninety to nothing about all he intended to do. The first hint of cool air was all the excuse they needed to walk home a little slower from fishing the river by the train tracks, Toby carrying the poles, Josh the tackle. It was a time for making plans.

But this September would be different. This September there would be no fishing under the trestle, no walks back home when even nightfall couldn't hurry them along. This year there had been the train.

Now the dirt under his toes turned crusty from the heat of the day, and the groves gave off the sharp, acrid smell of leaves, the smell of green.

No matter what, Toby was my best friend, Josh thought. *But, if he was your best friend, and you didn't know about this place in the groves, what else do you think you might not know?*

His stomach began this little exercise it had been doing lately. Squeeze. Give. Squeeze. Give.

And guess what? he wondered. *Toby knew people you never heard of, told them things, spent time at their house, promised to build a fence, and who knows what all else?*

Josh picked up a stick from the ground and

whacked it against the leaves of an orange tree.

If he didn't go back to that shack in the woods, Mattie would only think he had not wanted to finish the fence, and that was that. He thought of Mattie and flung the stick away.

At the line of trees that flanked his road, he swung up to a tall branch and looked his own house over. Quiet. Yeah. That's what it was like now. Quiet. He could feel it from there. Those rooms were made for two boys, him and Toby, not just one boy, not just him.

If Josh didn't go back to Mattie and Bess Ann's, they wouldn't call trying to find him. They didn't know him well enough to check up on where he was. They hadn't even done that with Toby, them not having a phone. He never had to worry about Mattie and Bess Ann again. He didn't have to build a fence.

Josh yanked off a leaf that tickled his cheek and shredded it.

But he should have told them. Toby is dead. He should have said so right off. Now Mattie and Bess Ann were waiting for him to come back. The same way they had waited for Toby. At that house in the groves, Toby was still alive. It seemed as though he would be as long as Josh didn't ruin it by telling Mattie and Bess Ann otherwise and making that the truth.

The last bit of sun lit on the chickweed below. This was the closest that Lakeland, stuck dead center in Florida, ever came to being cool in August. Josh raised his chin and held his hair off his face to catch anything that felt like a breeze.

He knew he would go back to that shack in the morning. He knew as surely as he knew that when the sun disappeared, bats would fly through the blue-gray dark. Toby was gone, and he had kept that from Mattie and Bess Ann. It was the worst thing he had ever done, and somehow he would have to make it right.

4
Nightfall

After supper Josh followed Daddy down the stairs to the basement. The smell of engine oil and sawdust rose through the darkness.

"Let's see what we've got here."

Daddy turned on the utility lamp that hung over his workbench. The light shone on Toby's chair, the one that had once held a baseball cap and cleats beside his bed, more recently an air gun and fishing tackle.

"Give me a hand, Josh, would you?" Daddy tugged at the arms and legs of the chair. "Is the wood cracked on that side?"

Josh stepped forward, but stopped short of the table.

"Two rungs broken." Daddy wiggled the foot rail. "Everything underneath is loose."

"Why is it down here?" Josh asked. "What are you going to do with it?"

Daddy didn't seem to hear. "I could sand it down. Reglue the joints. Have to replace some of the broken wood with oak."

Josh ran his fingers across a peeling place on the side of the chair. Tiny bits of red dusted his palm.

"Your momma might like it painted blue. We could put it by the wood stove in the sitting room." Daddy looked up all at once with new light in his eyes. "What do you say, Josh? We'll work on it together. Get it looking just right."

"No," Josh said. "It's fine the way it is." He turned away from his father's eyes and looked out the black slit windows of the basement as though he might see something there besides his own reflection. "It would look stupid painted blue."

His father stood still for a moment as if he were listening to the muffled, tapping sound of Momma's footsteps on the wood floor overhead.

"You're right," he said finally. "I don't know why I didn't see it. We'll give it a fresh coat of red, then. Get it in working order." Daddy laid a hand on Josh's shoulder, and Josh smelled his pine-tar scent. "A chair's no good if you can't use it."

Josh jerked away. "Put it back where it belongs." Toby's chair would never be right in the sitting room, holding a basket of cross-stitch threads. "Can't you see? It's not right to change it."

He ran up the stairs, his father staring after him. From his room, Josh could see the light in the woodshop. It burned long after he went to bed. He fell asleep watching a full moon rise over the filigree of trees outside his window.

Around midnight, he woke from a bad dream in a tangle of sheets. The moon was a great, round bowl of light.

"You all right, Josh?" Momma appeared beside his bed.

She rubbed his back in circles, as though he might be sick. "You know you can tell me anything you want to. Daddy, too. We've missed you this summer. You seem to always have somewhere to go." When Josh didn't say anything, she said, "How is Ritzy doing?"

"Good. He's real good. He's teaching me how to do a lay-up. We're both trying out for basketball." Josh sat up and swung his legs over the side of the bed. Trying out for the basketball team was something Toby wanted, not Josh. The lies were coming fast, as if someone had turned on a tap.

Momma looked toward the window and he saw from the moonlight coming in that she had a sad turn to her mouth. "I wish Toby could be here to see you. I bet he'd be proud. Trying out for the team," she said, as if she couldn't believe it. "I bet you make it, too."

She turned to him with a look Josh understood. Toby would never try out for junior varsity this fall the way he had planned.

Josh pushed himself out of bed and went to the door so he wouldn't see Momma's face. "I'm going to get some water."

Momma stood and smoothed down his sheets.

"I told Ritzy I would meet him at the Y at the crack of dawn."

"That sounds good, Josh," Momma said.

He could tell she believed him.

"We might go see a movie after that," he said.

"Real good." She laid a hand across his

cheek as she passed through the doorway. "'Night then."

"'Night." He waited till she had gone back to her room and shut the bedroom door before he moved.

It was true what they say about lying. The first time you do it is hard. The second time not so hard. He guessed the next time there would be nothing to it. The spaghetti he had for supper began to stir in his stomach.

He crept down the hallway. The linen closet door was the next one, then Toby's. It was closed, had been, since the accident. But Josh knew what was inside by heart: posters of teams and players on every wall, two dusty bookshelves that balanced a desk and an ancient typewriter, a terrarium that once held a garter snake, ribbons from basketball, an army fatigue jacket hanging on a hook above the door, and a box filled with yearbooks, foreign coins, a rusted cannonball, and a bag of hard candy shoved under the bed. Josh pressed his palm against Toby's door like a doctor with a stethoscope.

A moment passed. Nothing. He must be going crazy. What did he expect to happen?

When he heard a bed creak down the hall, Josh slipped back into his room before Momma or Daddy came out and asked what he was doing.

He turned on the radio beside his bed so he wouldn't think of Toby or Mattie and Bess Ann's house in the woods behind the orange groves.

The all-night disc jockey on WORG was taking requests. Three songs played before Josh was able to close his eyes and sleep.

5

Harmonicas, Paint, and Carving Knives

By nine o'clock, the sun overhead had baked a white glaze on everything. It had burnt away the haze in the field behind the house, and Josh's shoulders and neck besides. The fence posts were marked by ten. Six were sunk and cemented by two, but there were still a dozen more to do.

"I'm taking a break," Josh told Bess Ann.

He felt her eyes on him, heard her footsteps behind him as he moved into the shade of the stumpy porch footings.

"You like music?" Bess Ann pulled a transistor from her pocket and flipped through stations till she settled on one. "I really do."

She washed her feet in the tap, scrubbing her legs with her palms. "You know what my favorite musical instrument is? Harmonica."

Josh swiped at the sweat trailing like ants toward the waist of his jeans. He searched her face for any trace of coyness or teasing, but there was none, only that clear spring again.

"Toby can play anything. Did you ever hear him?"

"Plenty of times." The muscle beside Josh's mouth began to twitch.

He didn't want to talk to Bess Ann. He didn't want to know her. He wanted to finish the fence and be done with it.

'Well, do you?" Bess Ann asked.

"What? Play harmonica? No."

Bess Ann's hair was pinned in ribbons at the sides. Josh didn't know a girl his age who would be caught dead wearing her hair that way.

"Mattie's an artist. She paints."

"I saw the picture she did of you in the house yesterday," Josh said.

Bess Ann laid her hands on the grass. Her nails were chewed short, with bubble-gum-colored polish. "I don't play harmonica or paint."

"What does playing harmonica or painting have to do with anything?" Josh rolled onto his side and closed his eyes.

"Nothing, I guess," Bess Ann said.

"Look, my momma says everybody has a talent." Josh paced his words slow, like he was running, and this was his first lap around. "Maybe you just haven't found yours yet."

"Oh, I already know mine." Bess Ann ran into the chicken house and came back with a plastic shopping bag. She dropped a little wooden figure into Josh's palm. It was a perfectly carved chick. "That's Cotton," she said.

"She's my very own baby chick. There she is over there by the clothesline."

Josh looked in time to see a tiny puff of fuzz scoot into the flower border.

"I do rabbits and bobcats, too," Bess Ann said. "Even though I never seen one."

Josh ran his hand over the chips. Bess Ann's hands were strong looking, older than her face. And the carving was better than most he'd seen, maybe even the best.

"Wanna know how I do it? With this." Bess Ann pulled a pocketknife from her cutoffs and let the blade catch the sun.

"Hey. Be careful with that thing. Cut your hand off," Josh said. He gave the wooden figure back.

"Oh, I am. Else Mattie won't let me whittle no more." Bess Ann followed Josh's every movement with her stray-dog eyes till he couldn't stand it a minute longer.

"I've gotta get back to work."

Bess Ann slid the carving back inside the bag and ran into the chicken shed. When she came out, she wasn't carrying the bag. "Okay, ready," she said.

Josh stabbed the shovel in the ground. "I don't need any help . . . "

"I want to."

Josh felt heat building inside him. "Don't you have anything else to do? Feed your chickens or something?"

"No. I'm finished till Mattie needs me to set the table. And that's hours from now."

He would be stuck with her all day. Bess Ann would be after him to talk and listen and do things with her, just like at home. Momma's voice came singing in his ear: "Josh, how about a game of Scrabble? Josh, you want to ice the cake? Josh, come in here and listen to what Daddy says happened at the woodshop."

46

He walked a yard or two ahead to the next marker.

"Do you have one?" Bess Ann rolled the cuff at the hem of her jeans up to her knee to expose pale, freckled legs. "A talent, do you? You know, like your momma said?"

He turned so quick she almost bumped into him. "I already told you I don't. And I don't carve neither."

Bess Ann looked down and dug a toe in the dirt. She stood there till the place between them seemed filled with only what was left of his words.

"But I bet I've read more books than anyone you know." Josh cursed himself as he said it.

"Lucky," Bess Ann said. "I can't read."

Josh threw a shovelful of dirt to the side and looked at her. "Can't?"

She shook her head. "If I could, Mattie says

maybe I could go to school in town and ride the bus and all with the other kids."

"You don't go to school?" he asked. "You have to. It's the law."

Bess Ann shrugged. "I never lived nowhere long enough till Mattie took me in last April."

"I thought Mattie was your grandma."

"Mattie is my ma's kin, see? My ma and pop are pickers. Groves in spring. Apples in fall. Anyways, Ma said it would be better, you know, for me to stay with Mattie awhile. Then I wouldn't have to be moving all the time."

Josh shoveled more dirt from the hole. "Maybe Mattie could help you read some."

"Oh, she does. But I don't remember too good. Sometimes I forget the letters by the time we get at it again." Bess Ann peered back at the house as though what she was saying were only for Josh's ears. "But I sure wish I could go to school."

Josh thought of the quiet at his house, the same quiet Bess Ann probably had most times at hers. He studied her till her cheeks turned red and she looked toward the marigold pots on the porch. For the first time today, he thought she might be wanting away from him.

"It doesn't matter if you can't read," he finally said, picking up his shovel again. "You whittle."

"I think it matters," Bess Ann said.

"Lookit. I've got to work fast if I'm going to get in a swim before I go home."

"At the lake?" Bess Ann asked. "Can I go with you?"

Josh didn't say anything, just worked some more dirt out of the hole.

"Mattie will let me if I tell her you're going with me. Please, Josh, please?"

He wouldn't look at Bess Ann's face for fear

he'd feel bad and go soft. "No," he said. "I'm swimming out to the middle."

"I'm a good swimmer. I won't be no trouble," Bess Ann said. "Toby always took me."

Josh's stomach clenched, but he set his mind on the fence and ignored it.

"I doubt there'll be time now." He was mad at himself for not just saying flat no, for not keeping his big mouth shut in the first place.

"Don't worry, I'll help," Bess Ann said.

She worked a hundred miles an hour from then on, pushing her shovel into the post holes till sweat drained down her cheeks and soaked the neck of her T-shirt.

There wasn't much he could do to turn her back from that lake when he collected his things and said goodbye to Mattie. He started a fast walk through a grassy path in the direction of the water.

"Wait!" Bess Ann yelled, still pulling on her shoes. "Wait for me, Josh."

Josh began to run. When he reached the open stretch that led to the water, he saw to the west the dark woods where Toby and he had built their tree house. Now he knew why Toby always brought him there from the other side, by the lake path, where the marshes edged in on lichen-skinned oaks and palm trees covered with peeling sheaths. Those woods were shouting distances from Mattie and Bess Ann's house.

"I've got burrs," Bess Ann said as she caught up to him. She wiped at the soles of her feet and followed his gaze into the woods. "I wouldn't go in there. Mattie says it's a moccasin hole."

"Toby built a tree house there," Josh said. Right away, he wished he hadn't told her. Bess Ann already knew plenty about Toby that Josh never would. She had pieces of him that Josh could never get back.

He felt the sudden urge to sprint, and did,

throwing his roll of shoes and jeans onto the sand just before he hit the water.

By the time he heard Bess Ann swimming, he could tell from the slap of her arms that she was tired from the run. He swam out farther and floated on his back, watching the clouds passing across the sun turn the lake from blue to gray to green.

"I'll wait right here for you, Josh," Bess Ann yelled from chest-high. "I'm kind of tired."

Josh stirred the water with his arms. He wouldn't feel sorry for her. He wouldn't. Let her learn to leave him be.

"I'm glad you came to finish the fence," she said. "It hasn't been so much fun since Toby left. Mattie says I've been moping." She swirled a hand across the top of the water. "You're different than Toby, though, for being brothers."

Josh dropped his feet under him. "That just proves you don't know Toby very well. He and I are just alike. He and I like everything the same."

Bess Ann's lip quivered, and seeing it, Josh turned and waded hard for the shore.

"He won't be back from camp for a good while, anyway," he said over his shoulder. "So I wouldn't go counting on Toby for anything anytime soon."

"Okay. Are you mad, Josh?" Bess Ann called.

"No. I've just got to get home."

He heard her legs pushing the water aside as she followed him in through the grassy shallows.

"Toby used to say that, too," he heard her say behind him.

6

Ritzy Pays a Visit

"Ritzy stopped by here today," Momma said. "He wanted to know where you were."

When Daddy passed him ketchup for his French fries, Josh saw it. The look Daddy got when Momma asked him to let her handle something. Josh had seen it plenty.

Once last spring, he and Toby had ridden to the fairgrounds with Ritzy. As soon as they locked their bikes at the front gate, Toby hooked up with some girl from school. Turned out it was Ritzy who went with Josh on the rides. Toby finally showed up an hour after they were due home, and by the time they crept in the back door of their house, it was past midnight. Momma was waiting at the kitchen table. "You should know better than to worry us this way," she had said.

Daddy, leaning in the bedroom doorway, had jingled the coins in his pocket. When Josh had met his eyes, Daddy shrugged and disappeared into the dark, leaving him and Toby to Momma's lecture. But not before Daddy gave Josh the same look he had not sixty seconds ago.

"I thought you were meeting Ritzy in town this morning first thing. That's what you told me." Momma spooned out a helping of green peas for Josh. "But Ritzy seemed surprised to hear it."

"He did?"

"Yes." Momma pushed a slice of meatloaf onto Josh's plate, then Daddy's. "He certainly did. Then suddenly he remembered. Said he

better get down to the Y. He'd kept you waiting long enough, and off he went."

Momma stood over Josh, her hand on one
hip while her other hand balanced the fork
and plate.

"We must have missed each other," Josh
said. He took a bite and raised a shoulder like
he remembered Daddy had that night long
ago. "I never did see him."

"How was the movie?" Momma asked.

"It didn't work out," Josh mumbled.

"Quite a sunburn you've got there, son,"
Daddy said, his voice rising higher like it did
when he was ready to change the subject.

"Your hair is wet." Momma sniffed. "Have
you been in the lake?"

"Went with a friend," Josh said, studying
the cracks in his plate. Momma had collected
seventeen president's plates from Publix.
Thomas Jefferson had the same frown as
Momma did now.

"A friend," she said. "Do we know this friend?"

"Son, we know you're having a rough time this summer. That's no secret." Daddy folded his hands at the edge of the table. Calloused fingertips, yellowed from sanding and varnishing. "We're not trying to pry or intrude on your grieving — "

"I'm not," Josh interrupted. He couldn't help wondering how those beat-up hands could belong to the same man with such a gentle voice. "I'm not grieving."

"But it would be okay if you were," Daddy said. "Not that we would want that, but it would be natural." Daddy looked at Momma. "We're all having a rough go of this." He tapped Josh's hand with his fist.

Josh's backbone pressed into the rails of the chair. He didn't want to know what Momma and Daddy were feeling. He'd rather think about anything else but that. The expression on their faces said what they wouldn't — that Toby was gone, leaving a hole Josh could never fill.

"It's just that your mom and I wonder . . ." Daddy's voice was like listening to a car radio with the windows rolled down. Soothing. Almost like sleep, if Josh could just stop his words.

"We wonder why we have to find out what you're doing, what you're not doing, from Ritzy," Momma said. "Instead of from you. You're not grown, yet, Josh. We still need to take care of you. We can't look after Toby anymore. That's bad enough." Suddenly, tears rolled down her cheeks and spilt a dark trail by the buttons of her shirt.

Josh jumped to his feet, and his chair fell to the floor. He was a sand timer turned over.

Momma stared at the chair lying on its side. Daddy made a church and steeple of his fingers. It felt to Josh as though they might stay that way forever, with nobody talking or looking at each other.

He snatched up the chair and pushed it back into its place. He almost told them, then. The words welled up from deep down and they were close to pouring out. But he couldn't tell Momma and Daddy about the house in the woods. That would only lead to more questions.

"May I be excused?" he whispered.

Momma sat back down and laid her hands in her lap as though they were stones. Josh had to get out of that house.

"I'd like to be excused," he said.

Daddy nodded and Josh didn't wait for more than that to fly out the screen door and cut around through the back trees past the water tower to the groves.

There was still a half hour of light and he

intended to make the most of it. He walked fast to the clearing in the orange groves, where the woods had taken over for a hundred feet or so across its middle. An old pine log had fallen. Toby and Josh used to meet at that log when they wanted to talk about things they couldn't discuss at the house.

When Josh came around the corner, he saw an egret resting on the stump. The bird had dirty white feathers, and its wing tips, back, and head were as yellowed as Daddy's hands.

Josh had never seen an egret so far from Jessup's Farm. There, the birds usually had their pick of the fat, brown cows that chewed the soggy grass beside the lake. They lived off the grasshoppers and crickets that the cows stirred as they walked.

"Poor thing," he said. "You're hungry, huh?"

The bird looked straight at him and Josh realized how quiet the groves had become. Above him, the sky smoldered as red as a blown-out candle.

It was the kind of sailor's sky Josh had seen over the bay at Gran Evelyn's house in Wabasso, where he and Toby had spent a hundred afternoons hauling in oysters to shuck for supper.

Sometimes after they finished, he and Toby would try to find two halves of the same shell and fit them back together. When Josh placed his part of the oyster shell against Toby's and they couldn't tell it had been opened, they knew they had done it. It was a perfect thing again, whole.

But the last time they had been in Wabasso, Toby had said matching oyster shells was a kid's game. Since the accident, Josh had never tried again. Nothing had been whole since then, anyway.

Josh watched the egret on the log. "Go," he pointed. "You'll find it if you head that way. I bet some bull is switching himself to death waiting for you to show up."

The bird turned and looked in that direction.

"Shoo!" Josh ran toward the log. "Get going!" He waved his arms and the bird pushed into the air, stroking hard with its wings, barely missing the treetops.

"Very impressive."

Josh whirled around and saw Ritzy standing with his arms folded over his chest. His blond hair curled from under the rim of his Dodgers baseball cap.

A slow heat rose under Josh's cheeks. He could almost imagine Toby somewhere behind Ritzy, calling out, hidden by the dark line of trees.

"A regular Doctor Dolittle." Ritzy flashed his braces.

"Ritzy. What are you doing out here?"

"Just passing through," he said. "Came by to see you today. Your mom tell you?"

"Yeah, thanks for covering." Josh studied a crack in the lip of his dirty sneakers.

"Well." Ritzy stretched himself out along the length of the log. "I was just curious what it is I'm covering for, if you know what I mean."

Josh circled his knees with his arms. He could smell a grill going somewhere. Barbecued chicken. He remembered he hadn't eaten dinner.

"Thought you might show up at the gym. I'm getting good. Gonna whup you next time we play. Been swimming at Busse Creek some, too. Been waiting for you." He grinned at Josh and waited for him to talk, but Josh kept quiet. "Did I tell you James is playing for St. Martin's this fall? Found out yesterday. Marsha Gretsky thinks that is 'sooo wonderful'."

Ritzy smiled and batted his eyes. Josh couldn't help smiling. Then Ritzy turned his face toward the late, pink light. "You know, summer's about over, and I haven't seen anything of you since . . . well, for three months, anyway."

Josh knew what he had almost said. The last time he saw Ritzy was at the funeral. Just the thought of it brought back the smell of gardenias and perfume and cigarette smoke.

"I got things to do," Josh told him.

"That's not what your mom said."

"My mom. What did she say?"

"Relax, Josh. She's just worried about you, that's all. You've pretty much been in another dimension since . . . "

His voice slowed just a shade, enough for Josh to finish the sentence in his head. Since Toby died.

He skimmed a rock into the weeds. "It's

okay. You can say it." Josh made a fist of his fingers. "Did she send you down here looking for me? Is that what you're doing?"

Ritzy swung his legs to the ground and leaned toward Josh. "What I'm doing is trying to figure out where you are these days, man. That's all."

"I'm right here." Josh backed away. "I'm just here."

Ritzy held a hand to his head. Josh had seen him do it a million times. Pictures of Ritzy and Toby. Toby and Ritzy.

"Lookit. I gotta go." Josh half laughed, the kind that means no more questions.

"Josh. Listen. That's not all . . . "

Josh turned and walked fast. As fast as he could.

"I've missed you, Josh. It's not just you, you know," Ritzy shouted behind him. "It's not just you."

Josh didn't answer. He tried to believe the wind was blowing the wrong way and he couldn't hear a word, that Daddy was calling him home to get ready for bed.

He knew, as he hit the ground running, that tomorrow, when he went back to Mattie and Bess Ann's, he could almost believe there were places where Toby still lived. And Josh didn't want to change that, even for Ritzy. Even for a minute.

7

Learning Lizards

Mattie shook her head at the pile of apples Bess Ann had sliced and left sugared on the kitchen table. "Where'd Bess Ann go in such a hurry?"

"Said she had an idea," Josh answered.

"Good gosh. You'd think I was making a half-dozen pies. I guess I am now, at that." Mattie took out flour and butter and ice water to start more pie crusts. Her fingers moved as though they had done the chore a million times. Mattie poured and mixed and pinched and kneaded with care, the way Josh had seen her choose and mix her paints that afternoon while he worked on the fence.

"I don't know what we would have done if you hadn't happened along this summer," Mattie said. "Didn't know how dull it was for her till you came along."

Josh looked at a cut on his thumb. "I didn't mean to make trouble."

Mattie's gaze shifted from the filled pies on the counter to the kitchen window.

"It was bound to happen. I need to be making some plans for Bess Ann. I told Toby once that I meant for Bess Ann to be in school by now."

Josh turned away from Mattie and washed his hands in the cold water of the tap.

"She'd be happier. Learn to read, write. Maybe even make some friends."

"How about you, Mattie? Don't you ever feel like getting out of here?" he asked.

Mattie frowned and flattened against the counter. "I guess I do. But then I get into town and pick up supplies. Chew the fat with Mr.

McClelland at the art store or stop for a coffee at the counter. Truly, I work better without much company." The window framed a picture of the golden sky and everything under it — the fence, the yard, and thicket of pines. "I have Bess Ann, of course. And you. What else would I need?"

"Hey!" The door burst open and Bess Ann raced in. Her hair had fallen loose from the combs on the sides of her head. She held something behind her back, grinning at Josh like she had the best secret in the world.

When he smiled back at her, she held out her hand. He put a palm under hers, and she dropped something in it. Cool and hard. A chunk of wood.

"Going to teach you how," she whispered.

"Teach me?"

"To whittle." Bess Ann grabbed Josh's hand and pulled him toward the door.

"Now?" He looked at Mattie, but she just shrugged.

"Half hour till dinner. Josh, don't you think your parents might be worried where you are?"

"They're not worried." Ever since he knocked over his chair at dinner, Momma didn't ask where he was going anymore.

"Sure?" Mattie asked.

"C'mon." Bess Ann dragged Josh away before he had to answer.

The porch was all shaded, the garden long with shadows. When Josh sat beside Bess Ann, he felt the warmth of the sun still fresh in the boards beneath them. Bess Ann took a block of wood from her pocket and began to rub it. Then she put it up to her nose and sniffed. Licked it once.

"Bess Ann, cut it out." Josh tried to stop the impatience that slid into his voice. "What in the world are you doing?"

"Trying to figure out what's in it." Bess Ann studied the wood over her freckled nose. Her lips were pressed together in a tight seam. "Every time is different, even if the wood looks the same. Go on, feel it."

Josh rubbed the wood against his cheek. Even though nobody was there to see, he felt stupid. But when he sniffed, he thought of leaves and wood fern.

"Mine's a cat," Bess Ann said. "What's yours?"

She'd never be happy till he named something. "Lizard," Josh said.

"Never found a lizard." Bess Ann frowned. "Anyway, take your knife and just start to make tiny cuts. Like this. Away from you. If you take your time, there'll come a lizard."

Josh lifted the penknife Mattie had loaned him. He made his first cut along an edge. It peeled away like the skin of a green orange.

Bess Ann nodded. "That's right."

The wood felt warm and smooth where Josh's knife had been. He stopped more than once to see if it looked like anything. If he kept digging in so hard, his lizard would be nothing but a toothpick.

Bess Ann pulled her blade up and down the wood, and the next time Josh raised his head, he saw a sleeping cat in her hand.

He could feel a blister welling up under the tip of his thumb, but Bess Ann's concentration made him work harder, and before he knew it, the light was dim. Mattie was calling them in from the door, and a creature kin to a lizard lay at rest in his hand.

"I've got something I've been meaning to talk to you about," Mattie said.

They had just finished dinner — fried catfish, pole beans and tomatoes, watery iced tea, and apple pie.

Josh stopped sweeping the floor under the table. "You have?" Every time Josh saw Mattie lately, he dreaded this moment. He leaned the broom in a corner and stood behind the chair nearest the door.

"I'm going out to check the chickens." Bess Ann stuffed her mouth with a last bite of pie. "When Josh puts in that last piece of fence, I won't have no more worries."

Mattie pulled out a chair and motioned Josh to sit down. She poured him coffee, which he was not allowed at home. Now he welcomed its bitter taste.

"You know I grew up in a house full of boys. Three brothers." The reflection of Mattie's face was fuzzy in the silver pot. "Did I ever tell you that?"

"No," Josh said.

"I've gotten old so fast, I'd almost forgotten what fun it was." She poured cream into her cup from a cow-shaped pitcher.

"You're not old," Josh said.

Mattie sipped her coffee. "But having you and Bess Ann and Toby around this last year has made me not mind being old so much. That brother of yours sure can talk . . . " Mattie reached across the table and squeezed Josh's shoulder. "I'd like it if you talked a trifle more." She smiled. "But you're quieter than Toby."

Josh stroked the dark grain of wood that ran through the table. "I guess."

"I got no arguments with a quiet man. And a goodhearted one, double so. Came back to finish the fence." Mattie began to gather up the dishes. "And the way you are with Bess Ann . . . oh, yes, sir. We've been blessed since you came to us."

74

Josh's stomach seemed to wrap around something small and hard in his center.

"Now, Toby? Toby would talk about any-thing, . . . everything." Mattie laughed. "That boy loved to hear himself."

Talk, Josh thought. *Yeah, Toby could talk. And toe tap, and leg slap, and whistle, and snap fingers, and joke all day.*

"Bess Ann kept quiet when he was around. Guess she couldn't bring herself to get in the middle of all that conversation."

Josh shoved his napkin to his mouth. He couldn't tell Mattie that Toby hadn't told him anything about the talks he had with her. He couldn't tell her that, just this year, Toby was suddenly full of secrets. He had stretched far-ther than the sun, it seemed, leaving the boundary of their white house across the as-phalt road, moving beyond the people who lived inside it.

"But your being quiet and all, Bess Ann seems louder. You're the one who pulls words out of her," Mattie said. "How's he doing, anyway? Our boy?"

"Who?"

"Toby. Have you talked to him?"

"Not much." Josh's mouth was suddenly dry, but Mattie's brown eyes wouldn't leave his face. "Just once or twice after the rates go down at night."

"I see." Mattie leaned toward the window. "If I didn't call that girl in, I swear she'd stay out all night."

Mattie disappeared out the back door to call Bess Ann, and Josh was left alone in the quiet of the kitchen. Mattie's words banged around in his brain like pebbles in a tin can. He had to be so careful now to remember what he had told Mattie, what he had told Bess Ann, what he had said to one and not the other.

His eyes strayed to the wall of pictures. He took the thumbtacks out of a photograph of Bess Ann when she was little and studied the white spots of her cheeks, her missing front tooth.

All those words he had spun together were churning inside his head, out of control, like a twister.

He remembered the photograph Daddy had shown him once in the newspaper, the picture of a house after a tornado. All that was left when the storm passed was a single, narrow closet on a hill.

Under the picture was a caption that read in block letters LAST LEFT STANDING. For a long time after he had seen the picture, he would recall that tiny closet, the one thing that held firm in a mass of rubble. It had saddened him. He had not been able to forget it. Even then, as he stood in Mattie's kitchen, he could see the photograph clear as day in his mind.

Josh pinned the picture of Bess Ann back in place and pulled the faded curtain aside at the back door. Mattie was bringing in the last things from the clothesline by the shed while Bess Ann practiced the dunk shot Josh had taught her with rolled-up balls of socks. She saw Josh and waved.

A tightness crept through Josh's arms and legs. Soon, summer would end and he would be going back to school. He dropped the curtain closed before Bess Ann followed Mattie inside.

If he could give Bess Ann her own small closet, maybe he could go back to the way things were before he found Mattie's house in the groves. Maybe he could forget the way this whole thing had started.

Bess Ann washed her face in the kitchen sink, then turned to Josh, still dripping water.

"I don't know how Cotton can stand it,"

Bess Ann said. "I wonder if chickens die from heat. Do you think they could?"

Mattie began to fill the sink with hot water.

"Don't worry about the chickens right now, Bess Ann," said Josh. The sheer energy of his idea made Josh almost stand on tiptoe. "I'm going to teach you something, too."

Bess Ann wiped her face with one swish of her arm. "You're going to teach me something, Josh?" Her hair dripped water down the side of her neck. "What?"

"I'm going to teach you to read, Bess Ann McCall."

Mattie turned to Josh with soapy hands. "Well, whaaaattt . . . "

Bess Ann's face lit up with that joyful light Josh had seen in the front-hall picture, but this time he had made it happen. It was him, and that smile was all his. Suddenly, there was nothing in the world harder than trying to smile back.

8

Taking a Chance

Bess Ann balanced on the seat of Josh's Huffy while he pumped the pedals. They stashed the bike in some bushes beside the water tower, then sprinted over the railroad tracks and down a long corridor of slim streets.

"For gosh sakes, Bess Ann, keep your head down," Josh said when they reached the center of town.

"Why?"

"It's a game, I told you," Josh said. And he would be the loser if Bess Ann didn't stay out of sight.

"Let's go this way, Josh." Bess Ann pointed

to a string of shops. "They's pretty things in that window."

"No." He pulled her into the back alley of White's Appliance and Repair. "No, this way."

"But, Josh. I hardly ever get to come in town. I promised Mattie I'd tell her all about my adventure. The way things are going, I won't have nothing to tell her." Bess Ann's eyes shone with tears.

"First of all, this isn't an adventure." Josh looked side to side and ran, holding on to Bess Ann's arm, all the way down the alley to the side yard of the First Redemption Church.

"Second, if we don't get a move on, we'll have to start home before we ever get there."

He poked his head around the side of the building and scanned the sidewalk that butted the street all the way to the library. Two ladies pushed babies in strollers a block away.

"Almost there. Let's rest a minute," he said.

Bess Ann crossed her arms over her chest and stuck out her chin.

"Look, I promise I'll bring you back another time."

In the shadow of the church, Bess Ann slumped against a red brick wall. "Josh. Come feel how cool these bricks are."

"Yeah, okay." He told himself he would not let her get under his skin. "Now hush a minute and let me think."

Ever since he'd promised to bring Bess Ann to Lakeland to get a library card, Josh had been sorry. Not sorry because she didn't deserve it. Shoot, she'd been up every night for a week, studying and learning the words of the books he'd brought her from his attic. You'd have thought he was taking her to Disneyworld the way she'd been acting.

It wasn't those things. It was that he hadn't been in town all summer. Hadn't had to talk to anybody since the funeral, and didn't want to now. Especially since Bess Ann was with him.

Bess Ann jerked his sleeve. "I'm hungry."

"Here. Eat this." He handed her an apple and she began to chew around its top in choppy circles.

"Tell me how it will happen again, Josh. How will I get the card? What will I have to do?"

"Nothing. You won't have to do anything. They'll just give you one."

"Just like that. Are you sure?"

"I'm sure." He gave her a hard look, so she zipped up and started in on a second row of circles.

It was what Momma had said this morning that worried Josh most. When he came home after telling Bess Ann he would be taking her into town that afternoon, Momma's car was still in the carport. It was Wednesday, double coupon day, and Momma was usually first in line at Sure Buy and home by noon. He had counted on it.

"You're about the last person I expected to see," Momma had said when he walked into the kitchen.

Josh stood there with his mouth hanging open, as if he were holding up the doorway with his two hands, till she motioned him to sit.

"Want toast?"

He shook his head. The newspaper was scattered across the table and someone had been at it with a yellow marker.

His mother brought him a glass of orange juice and placed it in front of him. She brushed his hair out of his face before she sat down again.

"If you're wondering, I've decided it's time

I got myself busy. The way you have. And your dad."

Josh nodded.

"School starts next week," she said. "Hard to imagine summer is over." She smiled at him, then at her fingertips.

"I have to believe you're doing all right, Josh. I have to believe it because you haven't given me the chance to do anything about it if you're not." She took off her glasses and rubbed her eyes. "I know you miss him. I know it's hard whether you want to admit it or not. And I care about you enough to know I have to make some kind of start."

Josh started to duck away, but Momma laid a hand on his.

"So, when Doctor Milner said he could use a hand at the animal clinic in town — "

Josh sat upright, like a deer that has heard an unfamiliar sound.

"I said I was interested. I've got an appointment this afternoon. What do you think about your momma taking a job?"

Josh saw the smile on Momma's face but couldn't think of a word to say. It had been a long time since he had seen her look excited. But he hardly had time to notice how she looked like a kid who'd won a prize. His cheek worked back and forth as he studied the curved line of Momma's cheek. Momma and Bess Ann and he were all going to be in town at the same time.

"Don't you usually go to town in the morning?"

"Now Josh, when did you start noticing when I go into town?" Momma met his eyes before she took another sip of coffee, and Josh wandered out of the room.

That's when Josh knew he'd have to take the chance. He had to go to town today, before Momma wondered what he was up to and decided to find out. He would wait until Momma's car had been gone a good while. He would take only back roads and get in and out of the library as fast as he could. Seemed like all he did lately was try to undo what he set into motion.

He stopped outside Toby's door and squeezed the knob before he opened it. The room smelled slightly of sweat and watermelon bubble gum. Josh took a shark-tooth necklace from the corner of Toby's top dresser drawer, pulled it over his head, and dropped the pendant inside his shirt. He slipped out the door and waited until he heard his mother turn a page of the newspaper. She didn't look up as Josh passed the kitchen to leave. Maybe the necklace would bring him good luck again that afternoon.

"Did you hear me, Josh? Are we going to sit

here much longer?" Bess Ann stooped beside him. "Are you sleeping?"

"No." The women and strollers were past the library and almost to the park. "But let's run the rest of the way."

Bess Ann's face was already coloring from the heat. Her hair lay in the two neat braids Mattie had plaited this morning, although the sides were damp and curly with sweat as they raced up to the library doors.

Josh nudged Bess Ann in ahead of him, scanning each side of the road. Then they made their way to the long desk at the front. Only a few people were in line.

"May I help you?" the lady behind the desk asked.

Bess Ann smiled and stepped up to the counter. Josh recognized Mrs. Hansen as soon as she lifted her chin to look at Bess Ann through her bifocals. Momma and Mrs.

Hansen had sat over a cup of coffee just last week.

Josh ducked into a stack of books and heard Bess Ann say, "My name is Bess Ann McCall, I'm twelve years old, and I'm here to get my library card. See, I'm new and hope to start school. I'm learning how to read and done well enough to come in town without Mattie to loan out some books. My friend that's teaching me brought me, that's how I came to be here."

Josh rolled his eyes to heaven. *Lord, are you listening to me?* He squeezed his eyes tight. *If you'll just let me off this one time . . .* He opened his eyes then because he knew he couldn't make that promise. All his promises and lies seemed to be tied together like the tail of a kite, swinging longer and longer. He wasn't about to start lying to the Almighty.

He waited. Waited for Mrs. Hansen to say

she sure would like to meet the friend who brought Bess Ann. Point him out to me, she would say, and Bess Ann would turn and call his name. Josh. He could see the word form on her lips. Josh Harding, where are you?

As if she had read his mind, he saw Bess Ann turn. He held himself low, right next to the musty smell of "American Biographies" and prayed nobody else could hear his own heart as he waited for that long kite tail to get snagged and come spinning down around him.

9

Surprise Meetings

"The library will be closed in fifteen minutes," a voice boomed from somewhere overhead.

From the "Large Print" shelves, Josh did a full sweep of the room but still didn't see Bess Ann. Mrs. Hansen had led her back to the children's section over an hour ago. A lady with red, curly hair stood where Mrs. Hansen had, stamping cards, helping a man in a business suit check out, then two girls in plaid jumpers.

The red-headed lady must have felt Josh's stare because she looked up and smiled. It was the same smile she had given Bess Ann when Mrs. Hansen had turned to her and said, "Did you hear that, Dottie? She's here for her first library card. This little lady is learning to read."

After that, everybody standing there, even the man fixing the copy machine had started patting Bess Ann's back and shaking her hand like she'd won the state lottery. A second later Mrs. Hansen had marched her away. Josh hadn't seen her since.

He knelt on the floor and peered through a gap in the magazine racks. Footsteps tapped up behind him. He twisted around.

"What are you doing down there?" Bess Ann asked.

"Never mind that." Josh jumped to his feet. "Do you have the card?"

"Here it is. Feel. It's still warm."

"Well, you sure took long enough to get

it." He pulled down his Seminoles cap, hooked his hand around her arm, and headed for the side door.

"Wait." Bess Ann shifted her books onto one hip and raised an eyebrow. "You almost made me drop them."

"Come on, Bess Ann. We've gotta go." Josh shouldered his way ahead of her toward the sidewalk. "Library's closing."

"Mizz Hansen . . . that's the lady what gave me my card? Anyway, she says she would consider it an honor to help me with my reading. Since Mattie told me you'll be starting school and all, I told her yes."

They ran behind the church again and started down the alley behind Main.

"I'd say you are doing just fine without any help from me," Josh replied.

The air was suddenly sweet and light. He took Bess Ann's books and put them in his backpack. They, he, had made it. He wanted to jump three feet straight up and yell.

Made it through town without running into a soul. Made it into the library and gotten Bess Ann her card. Made it, and now he was home free.

"Hey," a voice called from behind. "Hey, Josh Harding."

The pleasure of the last minute disappeared as quickly as the sun in a summer storm. Panic rose like thunder and pulled the hair on his neck away from his skin.

"Josh." A hand hit his shoulder. "You getting too good for your old friends?"

He whirled around. It was Ritzy. Something inside his throat made it impossible to swallow. "Hey," he said.

Bess Ann turned around and squinted at Ritzy for a minute. Then she began to jimmy something from her front pocket.

"I thought I saw you earlier, but I wasn't

sure it was you," Ritzy said. "Who's that?" He shifted his cap onto the back of his head and nodded at Bess Ann.

Josh couldn't unhinge his lips.

"Bess Ann McCall," Bess Ann said. "I've got me a new library card and money for a soda." She held up the library card in one hand and the coin she'd been after in the other.

"Uh-huh." Ritzy looked from her to Josh.

"I'm a friend of Josh's, if you're wondering." Bess Ann dove her hand back into her pocket. "Toby's, too."

Josh caught Bess Ann's eye and gave her a sharp look, but not before he saw Ritzy take a short step back.

"We're kind of in a hurry. Aren't we, Bess Ann?"

"No." She gave Josh a puzzled look.

"Maybe we could go get a soda at Kelly's," Ritzy said.

Toby, Ritzy, and Josh had always bought a

drink from the machine at Kelly's and watched who pulled up to the pumps from the front curb. It was tradition.

"Seems a shame not to since you're here," Ritzy said.

"Got it!" Bess Ann held another quarter up to her eye.

"Nope. Can't. Not today."

"Please, can we, please, Josh? Mattie won't care if we're late. Look, I've got fifty cents," Bess Ann said.

"No." Josh shot a side glance at Ritzy. "Sorry, Ritzy, we're way late already."

Ritzy nodded to Bess Ann, then pulled Josh aside.

"Well, then," he said, "how about riding with me over to the creek tomorrow? Maybe do some fishing?"

Bess Ann had raised herself on tiptoe to pat a black-and-white alley cat that sat on the stone wall beside some trash cans, but all at once she stood still.

"You're Ritzy?" Her eyes opened wide. "Weellll. Toby talked about you all the time." She grinned a minute, then the grin disappeared. "He told me you traded him a torn baseball card once. That wasn't very nice."

"Hush, Bess Ann," Josh said. "That's not your business."

When he turned back, Ritzy's expression told Josh everything he needed to know. Ritzy was on to something but wasn't about to ask Josh outright. Instead, as if maybe Ritzy were playing cards and held all the good ones, he said, "Tomorrow morning. I'll ride my bike over at eight or so."

"I don't think so," Josh said.

Ritzy stroked his cheek and studied Bess Ann. "Why not?"

Bess Ann rattled the change around in her

closed hand. Now she was squinting back at Ritzy, too, the alley cat circling her legs in a crazy figure eight. "I'd like to see you play basketball sometime. Josh says you're better than him, but I doubt it," she said.

Ritzy narrowed his eyes, as if Bess Ann were a sentence he had to read over and over again to understand.

Josh shuffled his feet. He raked his hair with his fingers. He guessed he could have done a handstand and Ritzy wouldn't have taken his eyes off Bess Ann.

"Do I know you?" Ritzy asked.

Before Bess Ann said something Josh couldn't put right, he stepped in front of her.

"Okay," Josh whispered. "I'll meet you at eight, but no questions." Then he raised his voice. "Only we've gotta go now. Like I said, we're late."

Bess Ann looked back over her shoulder as

Josh pulled her down the alley. "Bye," she yelled. "Bye, Ritzy."

Josh walked even faster.

"Come meet Mattie sometime."

Josh waited till they got across town to buy Bess Ann an ice cream at a place he'd never been, hoping he wouldn't run into anyone else he knew. Then, they looked in the window of a florist shop, where Bess Ann used her piggy-bank money to buy Mattie a violet in a white pot.

The whole way home, Bess Ann sang in Josh's ear from the seat of his bike.

"I got it," she yelled to Mattie from the dirt road in the groves, waving her library card over her head like a trophy and holding the flowerpot under her other arm.

Mattie clapped till Bess Ann reached the porch steps.

"And I said thank you, just like you told

me," Bess Ann told Mattie. "Is Cotton all right?" She shoved the flower in Mattie's hands and ran off behind the house to look for the little creature.

"Josh, you've done a wonderful thing," Mattie said. "She's proud as punch." She set the violet on a table by the porch swing. "Can you stay? Black-eyed peas and rice."

"Thanks, but not tonight. My mom got a job." He jogged up the road toward the groves.

"Sweet dreams, then." Mattie's voice was like the songs the birds called from the thick, grown-together lawns at the top of the trees.

It wasn't till he was back in the groves that Josh realized he had forgotten to tell Bess Ann he wouldn't be back the next day. They'd have to wait to finish the fence.

For the first time in a long while, going home didn't seem so bad. Different, maybe.

Like coming home from vacation, walking into your house and seeing it new.

Daddy had started to talk about baseball scores, and Momma might have her own news to tell.

Besides all that, he was going fishing. He hadn't spent a whole day with Ritzy in a long while. Hadn't been in about forever. He wondered how he'd explain Bess Ann to Ritzy, or what he could say to keep Ritzy from ever asking. His mind was working overtime, and he was in a hurry. He didn't even look back.

10
Old Times

Josh followed Ritzy through the knee-high grass, leaving a trail slick as a snail's behind them. When they reached the place where Busse Creek bent back on itself, Josh set down his tackle box and fishing pole. It was the same place where Toby claimed to have caught the biggest trout in Polk County last summer.

"This is it." Ritzy dropped his gear by the creek bank.

A red-winged blackbird darted from a branch overhead and swept across the water.

"What's the late-breaking news at the Harding house?" Ritzy asked. He tied off a hook at the end of his line and waded into the creek.

"My mom got a job," Josh said.

Ritzy cocked his head. "No lie?"

"Veterinary assistant." Josh threaded a kernel of corn onto his hook. "Hours are decent. Seems real happy about it."

"My mother is redecorating. Remember? She does this every time school starts." Ritzy jerked the line on his fishing pole to the side. It went slack until the flow of water caught and tightened it again. "My father says by the time James graduates, there'll be a couple dozen layers of wallpaper in our kitchen."

He grinned, and Josh fiddled with his hook. There was a time when he and Ritzy had talked like this, but now it seemed like ancient history. Still, he knew if he didn't say something, Ritzy would start asking questions about Bess Ann.

"You ready for high school?" Josh asked.

"Ready as ever." Ritzy arched an eyebrow. "Ready to show that junior varsity team what they've been missing."

It was so much like something Toby would say, Josh laughed. He took his fishing pole to the edge of the creek and cast his line. Currents moved under the water, giving the impression of a long green snake gliding in the sun.

"When do your practices start? I want to come see that killer Harding hook shot," Ritzy said.

"I haven't played since the last time we went one-on-one."

"Man, you better get going," Ritzy said. "You realize there's only a week left till school starts? How you figure to be ready for September tryouts?"

"I'm not going out for the team."

"What?" The tip of Ritzy's pole almost dropped underwater. "When did you decide this?"

Josh wasn't sure when. But as soon as the words came out he knew it was long ago.

"No great loss," he shrugged. "I spent most of the season on the bench anyway." Ritzy was still gaping, so he kept talking. "I'm thinking I might try out for cross-country this year."

"Cross-country?" Ritzy waded back toward shore and set his pole into the crook of a tree. "You hate to run."

"Yeah, I know I used to," Josh said. Ritzy dropped onto the bank beside him. "But it's different now. I've done some running over the summer." Back and forth from his house to Mattie's place in the groves. But Ritzy didn't know any of that.

"Grew your hair out, too, I noticed." Ritzy aimed his heel like a hoe into the dirt. "What else have you been doing this summer I don't know about?"

Josh felt his breath catch high in his throat.

It was the question he had been avoiding since Ritzy had knocked on his door that morning.

Smudges of white clouds and green pines reflected across the wide creek and into the grainy, sallow shore water. Like Mattie's watercolors, the trees, the sky, even Ritzy's red shirt blurred, making each shape a part of another.

Josh turned to see Ritzy squinting up at him. Waiting, that's what he was doing. Waiting for Josh to tell him things. Answers that weren't really answers. Or more lies, like the ones that rose and tumbled under the surface of the truth.

Ritzy cleared his throat. "Hey, if it's that hard . . ."

When Josh focused hard enough, the sky and the water in front of him became two hinged halves, like oyster shells. Josh couldn't pretend anymore. He wanted to fit the parts of his life together and make them into one whole thing again.

"See, I met this woman. Mattie McCall. You know her?"

Ritzy shook his head, and something in Josh lifted away on wings. Even Ritzy hadn't known Toby's secret.

"And Bess Ann — you met her yesterday. They live way out in the groves. Toby started a fence for them. I've been finishing the job."

"Toby." Ritzy broke a stick across his knee and flung it into the water. "It still makes me mad, you know it?"

Josh looked away, his heart pounding.

"Nobody but him would have taken that tunnel. Nobody else would have been that crazy."

Josh stared at the river till his eyes stung with tears.

"It's funny, man." Ritzy's voice seemed as though it might snap like the stick he had thrown into the water. He stood with his hands on his hips and talked to a place on the opposite bank as though someone were there listening. "People expect me to be like him, you know? Because we were tight."

"You don't have to be anything," Josh said. Maybe Ritzy thought Josh expected him to be like Toby. The same way Josh thought Momma and Daddy expected it of him. "Not for anybody. I mean it."

For a minute, the sound of crickets in the brush filled the silence.

"Never been to a cross-country meet," Ritzy finally said. "Guess it's time."

All at once, Josh's line yanked hard. He didn't move. He was wondering what Toby would say if he were there.

"You've got one, Josh!" Ritzy jumped to his feet. "Bring it in."

Josh began to pull and reel as the line zigzagged through the water.

The fish jumped ten feet in front of him. It was a beauty, silver as sun on water, and spotted the color of river mud. Josh reeled till he could see the dark circle of the fish's eye, the frantic pulse of its gills as he drew it up toward the surface.

"He's the biggest one I've ever seen," Ritzy yelled. "Bigger than Toby's!"

Josh steadied the fish and unhooked it. The fish writhed inside his fingers. Josh opened his hands and it was gone.

"What did you do that for?" Ritzy asked.

Josh yanked his shirt over his head and dove into the swirling water of the creek. He looked up in time to hear Ritzy let out a whoop and jackknife off the bend.

"Freezing," Ritzy yelled when he surfaced. "Doesn't it feel great, Josh?"

It surprised him, but it did feel great. The

tightness he had felt all summer loosened a notch.

Ritzy spun a handful of water in Josh's direction, and Josh dove to pull Ritzy's feet out from under him.

For a minute, they were the same two boys they had been every other summer. For a little while, not even a train could come between old friends, and Mattie and Bess Ann had never existed.

11

Search Parties

"Bess Aannnnn. Bess Aannn." Mattie's voice burst into the air like a bevy of quail.

Josh's mind was on the day before, fishing with Ritzy, goofing around like old times, even though a quiet now and then had reminded both him and Ritzy that Toby wasn't there. If Josh hadn't been so busy thinking, he might have heard it sooner, before his feet found the rough grit of the road.

"BESS ANNNNN."

Something about Mattie's voice told Josh she wasn't calling Bess Ann in for lunch. Something about it made him stop a split second before his legs could move.

Then he bolted down the road, past the lines of beans and tomatoes and onions, to the house.

"Bess Annnnn!" Mattie's voice again. But now it had an edge of panic he hadn't heard earlier.

"Mattie, where are you?" Josh stood in the back yard by the chicken house. It was strange to be there with no one around.

"Here!" A cry came up from the groves on the other side of the tool shed. "Here, over here, Josh."

When Josh saw Mattie, he knew whatever was wrong was worse than he had thought.

It reminded him of another day, when he had come inside from shooting hoops with Ritzy and seen Momma, turned away from him, phone beeping in her lap. The contents of her purse lay spilt beside her chair, but Momma hadn't moved to pick them up.

"What's wrong, Momma?" Josh had asked. He stomped on a penny still rolling across the floor.

A dull light, like the last bit of a match, flickered inside his mother's eyes. And something else Josh had never seen before, something he later recognized as pain. Josh covered his eyes at the exact moment Momma said the words, "It's Toby."

Now Mattie's eyes were lit with the same pain. "It's Bess Ann. She's gone." Mattie brushed the hair off her forehead. The fine dirt stirred up by the tillers streaked her face.

"Why would she do that?" Josh tried to picture Bess Ann wandering in the groves, but he couldn't. It didn't make sense.

"Cotton," Mattie said. "She must have gotten out last night. Bess Ann couldn't find her this morning when she went out to feed her." Tears made Mattie's eyes seem faded. "I told her looking for that little thing would be like trying to find a needle in a haystack, but she must have run off when I went in the house."

She held her head against her dirty wrists. "I should have known she wouldn't give up."

"Mattie, we'll find Bess Ann. I promise." He wrapped an arm around her narrow shoulders. "You go that way." He pointed to the groves in front of the woods. "I'll look behind, back by the lake."

"All right." The shakiness fell out of Mattie's voice. "But if we haven't caught sight of her by noon, I'm going to notify the police."

Josh ran till he found the path through the high grass and live oaks that led to the lake. He didn't worry about snakes or consider cutting through the field, which was farther but easier on the legs. He didn't think of anything, except Bess Ann out there alone.

"Bess Annnn!" From somewhere far away, Josh heard Mattie's voice like an echo.

"Bess Ann, it's me, Josh!" Only the sound of a motorboat on the lake answered.

He raced to the shore where they had gone to swim. In one direction, the shore thinned till it petered out and turned into groves. In the other direction were the dense, live oak woods and marsh.

Josh called Bess Ann's name again, but the wind stripped it away.

Then he saw a piece of wood on the ground. It was different from the gnarly, dark wood that washed up on the shore. He picked it up. It was one of Bess Ann's carvings, this one the start of a bird. It lay on top of the sand, not buried as it would have been if it had been there awhile.

Josh slipped the wood into his pocket. Bess Ann couldn't be far away.

He looked off into the dark, hunkering woods. Would she go in there alone? If Bess Ann had found Cotton, she would have gone home by now.

And if she hadn't, like he figured, she was upset. Sick, maybe. Things like losing something happen all at once. They don't take time for you to warm up to the idea.

His bare toe found the sharp point of a rock. The sand blossomed red.

To make matters worse, he hadn't been around when Bess Ann lost Cotton. He hadn't finished the fence. He'd been off baiting hooks with Ritzy. Having a fine time. Maybe she had worried about him. Maybe she thought he wasn't coming back.

A long tangle of Spanish moss hit Josh in the face. He was in the part of the woods where the trees were thicker, more spread out and squat from dim light. The rotten-egg smell of the marsh prickled his nose. He could see the cattails and hyacinths that fringed the lake's blue water.

The tree house emerged from the center of the woods. Josh saw the blocks Toby had nailed along one side of the trunk so they could climb. Suddenly there seemed to be nothing but the sound of Josh's breath drawing in the air.

He had the feeling he might walk and walk and never reach that oak. He wondered if his legs would give out with weariness, or fear, long before he reached it. Then there he was, staring at the deep-etched bark.

"This is the surprise I told you about," Toby had said.

It was the first time Toby had brought Josh to the tree in the woods.

"This?" Josh looked around at the gray branches of live oaks hung with moss and spiky air plants. "It's so dark back here."

"That's what's good about it." Toby

117

jammed his hands on his hips. "It's perfect. This is where we'll build our tree house."

Josh heard scratching noises in the ferns and tall marsh grass that might have been snakes. He breathed in the smell of rotting wood. He'd never come to this place without Toby, that was for sure.

"Why not closer to the house?" Josh had said.

Toby gave him a disgusted look.

"How about in that thick stretch of groves by Jessup's field?"

"People can spot you there. They can find you if you're not careful," Toby said. "But nobody would figure to look for you here. Nobody. Now would they?"

"I guess not," Josh said.

"This will be our secret place," Toby said. "Where you can be alone whenever you want." He grinned and gave Josh a wink as though he had already decided.

Josh didn't smile back because he knew it wasn't him Toby was looking out for. It wasn't Josh who wanted to be alone.

Toby walked around the perimeter of the tree. "I'll put blocks up the back side."

Josh kept quiet. If he squawked, Toby might not bring him next time.

"Cut a square out of the floor to get in. It's going to be perfect. Trust me."

Josh stared up at the place where Toby had pointed that afternoon. The opening in the floor of the tree house seemed higher than it had the times he'd come with Toby. Josh's hands and legs wouldn't stop shaking. He wasn't sure he could make it up the tree, but there was only one way to find out, and he had to do it. He shoved himself onto the first foothold and began to climb.

12

The Tree House

A piece of twig dropped past Josh's shoulder. He waited midway like a woodpecker on the tree.

"Bess Ann?"

He climbed the rest of the way and stuck his head through the splintered opening of the tree house floor. There in a corner was Bess Ann, head bent into her knees, hands pressed over her ears as though she expected to hear a gunshot.

Josh pulled himself into the tree house and laid a hand on Bess Ann's shoulder. She only wrapped herself into a tighter knot. Toby's initials carved into the board beside her made a wave of nausea pass through Josh.

"Bess Ann, I'm sorry." He said it as quietly as he could, like a secret. "Sorry about Cotton."

"Oh, Josh, I should have been watching better. She got out that corner of yard we hadn't fenced, and then she was just gone."

Josh squeezed closed his eyes. He pulled himself into the corner beside her and studied the cuff of her shirt he had watched Mattie embroider not a week ago with tiny flowered vines.

Bess Ann raised her face. Her nose was red and her eyes were shiny. Briars and bark and beggar's weed tangled her hair. "Then I came here." She rubbed her nose with the back of her hand. "Remember you told me once?"

"Weren't you scared of snakes?"

"I was scared before." Bess Ann shrugged.

"But it's not so bad here. Anyway, what difference do snakes make now? I don't have my Cotton no more."

Josh suddenly wished he were half as brave as Bess Ann. Half as real.

"Mattie worried?" Bess Ann asked.

"Didn't you know she would be?"

"Oh, Cotton," Bess Ann rocked back and forth against her knees. "I can't believe I can't have her no more."

When Josh looked in her eyes, the hurt was right there on top, like the trout Ritzy and he caught yesterday, not hiding like some catfish underneath everything. Not like his.

"I wish I could make it morning again. I'd never let Cotton out of my sight," Bess Ann said.

"You couldn't watch over her all the time, Bess Ann. You did your best." Josh traced Toby's initials, like veins in the wood, with his fingertips. He thought of the train flying out from the tunnel, taking Toby by surprise as he raced home from practice, late as usual. "Sometimes things happen for a reason you or me can't figure."

"Have you ever had that happen, Josh? To something you cared about, I mean?"

Josh leaned over the side of the tree house. From where he stood, the marsh, once frightening, seemed fragile and wild and perfect. It wasn't so bad, only different from what he was used to. Everything took getting used to, it seemed.

"You can tell me if you want," Bess Ann said. "If I were you, I would tell."

Josh lowered his head. He could almost see the steam rise from the ferns and rotting logs below, disappearing into the treetops and above, curling higher till it became part of the free blue sky.

"Josh." Bess Ann's fingers were on his back. "You don't have to. You don't. I'm so dumb sometimes I can't hardly stand it."

"Don't ever say that," Josh said. "There's nothing wrong with you, hear me?"

Bess Ann sighed and lowered herself through the opening in the floor of the tree house. "Josh?" She placed a hand beside his. "I'm going to miss her, though."

"I know," he said.

As he followed her down the ladder, he knew he would have that expression on Bess Ann's face imprinted on his brain forever, like the narrow closet left on the hill.

They started for the house, first in a walk, then in a run. Josh couldn't stop. Bess Ann panted behind, trying to catch up. He waited till he heard her footsteps before he raced forward again and again, to the place outside the fence.

124

"You go on, now," Josh said, when she reached his side. "Go let Mattie take a look at you." He pushed Bess Ann forward with one hand.

"I'll bet she's awful mad at me."

"She's not," Josh said.

"Aren't you coming?" Bess Ann asked. Her eyes rested on the shady place on the porch where Mattie always set up her easel.

"No." He wiped his hands down his shorts, brushed the hair away from his face. "You go ahead."

He watched Bess Ann walk through the yard and Mattie fly down off the porch to fold her into the tight circle of her arms. Then Josh made a run for the groves. Though pain rose inside him, his breath was even and his feet rose and fell as if they might continue forever. As if the act of running could settle a mighty storm into rain.

13

Late September

Beyond the wide-set trees of the groves, past the road and the smell of onions from the garden, Josh heard a voice rise, sweet and shaky. Mattie's voice.

He slipped behind a tree and watched her hang some canvases in the shade to dry. Tried to see her like a stranger would, like he had the first time he'd seen her, an old lady with saggy clothes singing only half good, but he couldn't. Mattie was too much a friend to look at her that way ever again.

"You just going to stay there spying all day? I was wondering when we would see you around here again." Mattie wiped her hands on her jeans, threw a sweater over her shoulders, and walked down the porch steps, past the marigolds Bess Ann had planted. "I was just going out to check the garden. Won't be long before there's nothing left. Come hold the basket for me."

Josh slid out from behind the tree and followed the path to the place where she stood. "Mrs. Hansen from the library took Bess Ann to see a play at the Civic Center. I thought Bess Ann would die before the woman come for her." She stopped all at once and squinted hard at him. "Got a haircut, did you?"

"Ritzy's father got his hands on me." Josh rubbed the place on the back of his neck that his hair used to cover.

Mattie nodded and knelt to pull a clump of weeds from the rows. He stared at the top of her head, blurry in the last sun.

"Mattie, I've got something to tell you." He felt his cheeks go hot though she hadn't turned her eyes to him yet. She didn't look up at all, just kept working over the rows of squash. "Something important."

"Look at this, Josh. Look how strong these squash vines are. These plants have grown some of the best vegetables I've ever seen. You take these home to your momma and daddy." She stood and handed him what she had gathered.

"Mattie — "

"But good as they are," she said, tapping a finger against his shirt, "it's real easy for bugs to bore in." She picked a tomato and handed him one. She rubbed hers on the front of her shirt and took a bite. "Just one can take your whole crop. Make the whole mess sick."

"Mattie, about Toby." Josh was talking too fast, spitting out the words. "He won't be coming back." Mattie kept her eyes on him. "He won't be coming back at all."

"I know." She eased herself to the ground. "I heard that."

"You did?"

"The day I went in to pick up canvases, right after you first come here, I asked the people in the art supply store in town if they knew of you." She puckered her mouth. "I found out then, Josh, about Toby, about the train." She cupped her hands around her knees and stretched her arms and body away. "I've been wondering when you would tell me yourself . . . if you would," she nodded, "and now you're here."

"Does Bess Ann know?" Josh asked.

"No. But she will. I'll tell her."

"She'll be mad with me," Josh said.

"For a while, maybe." Mattie's hand patted his. "Bess Ann don't stay mad long."

The hand over Josh's was as spotted as the underside of the squash. "How about you, Mattie?"

"I've had time. It's passed. But I wondered how big a hurt a boy could have to keep such a secret. Now I think I know how big."

"I want to finish the fence before Bess Ann comes home." Josh put his hand on the figure in his pocket for the hundredth time since he'd finished it yesterday. "Will you give her this for me? It's not as good as hers, but . . . it's Cotton."

Mattie took the carving. "If you promise to come see her yourself real soon."

Josh nodded.

"Go ahead on," she said, pointing in the direction of the chicken shed. "You know where everything is."

Mattie walked toward the steps of the house. The screen door slammed as he rounded the corner. He took the last of the chicken wire and a handful of nails to the last two posts and nailed one end shut.

The nails punched in easy. He unrolled the wire and stretched it tight to the last post. Maybe by next spring Bess Ann would be ready for a new chick and that one would be safe, as safe as anything can be from unexpected turns.

Mattie came out to the back stoop and switched on the light. She walked over to where Josh stood and handed him an old sweatshirt. "Weather's cooling," she said, rubbing her arms and tilting her head back to watch the swallows scribble the sky. "The change has come so fast. All in a month, it seems. Summer's already a shadow. I'm going in."

She shook her head, then stopped on the top step of the house. "You'll stay for pie, won't you? Tell me about school. Bess Ann won't be back for a while yet."

"Sure," Josh said. "Just one more to go."

He picked up the last nail, held it to the wood, and pounded hard. He stopped before he drove it in and breathed in the smell of dirt and pine, and from a place far away, the marsh beside the lake.

Then he closed his eyes and hammered once, hard, bending the nail to the side and into the wood, to make the strongest bond he could before he went inside.